0

Wish
you were here

D0453003

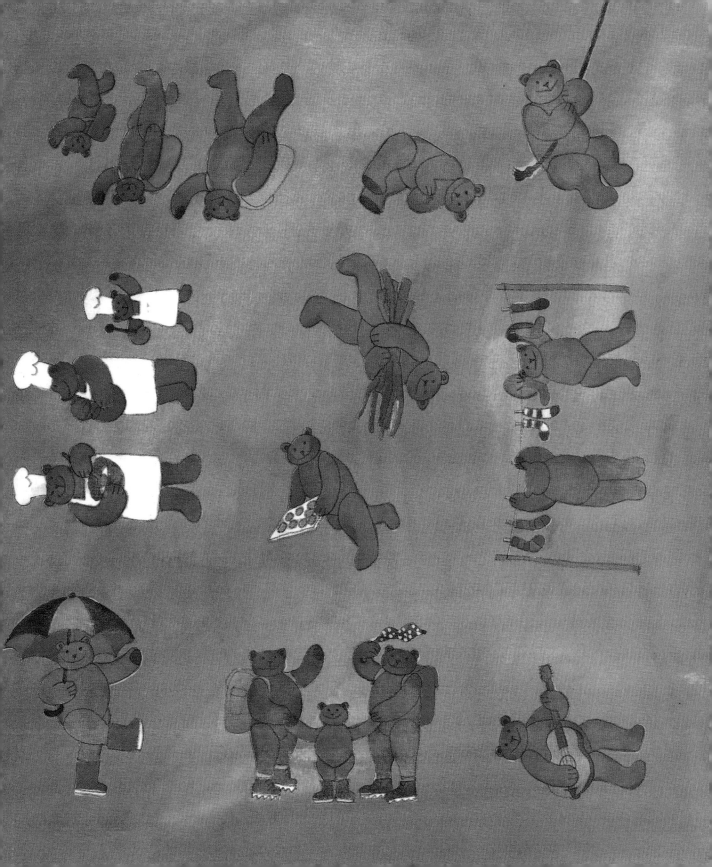

A Red Fox Book

Published by Random House Children's Books
20 Vauxhall Bridge Road, London SW1V 2SA

A division of Random House UK Ltd
London Melbourne Sydney Auckland
Johannesburg and agencies throughout the world

7 9 10 8 6

First published by Hutchinson Children's Books 1994

Red Fox edition 1996

Printed in China

RANDOM HOUSE UK Limited Reg. No. 954009

ISBN 0 09 938371 3

Wish
you were here

Martina Selway

Red Fox

London   Sydney   Auckland   Johannesburg

For Edna and Ted Price

Rosie is going on the school camp holiday.
Mum says she'll love it.
Grandad says she'll love it.
Aunty Mabel says she'll love it.
Rosie would rather stay at home.

Dear Mum,
   The minibus was very bumpy and I felt sick.
The driver stopped the 'bus, but when I got out
I felt better so we started off again. Then
Sarah felt sick.
Miss West said, "Let's all sing a song."
Sarah's face went funny and white, then
she <u>was</u> sick. It went all over my new
trainers.
I don't want to go to camp.

Love from
        Rosie

Dear Grandad,
    When we got to the camp it was raining and everywhere was muddy. Danny Fisher pushed Roland and he slipped into a huge puddle. He was covered in mud.
Mr Granville said, "Rule number one: don't get wet! It's difficult to dry things out when it's raining."
I think Roland was crying.
I don't like Mr Granville.
Love from Ginger Nut.

Dear Aunty Mabel,
   We are staying in this big smelly old cabin because it's too wet to sleep in the tents. I'm sharing bunks with Sarah but I don't mind because she's brought lots of biscuits with her. Danny kept trying to scare us. Miss Jones said, "Stop making those silly noises, Danny. You're not frightening anyone." But we were frightened.
I don't like it in here.

Love Rosie.

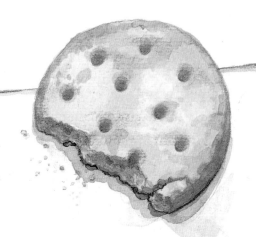

Dear Mum,
    When we woke up it was still raining. The boys helped to cook breakfast and it was awful. My egg was too runny. Afterwards we walked a long way through woods to visit an old Mill. On the way Danny wouldn't stop climbing trees. In the end he got stuck. It took ages to get him down. Mr Bennet said, "If you don't behave yourself Danny, you'll be sent home." We kept taking the wrong path. I wish I could be sent home.

Love from R.

Dear Grandad,
    The old Mill was brilliant. We watched corn being ground up to make flour. Everyone there was dressed up in old-fashioned clothes and looked very funny. Afterwards they gave us a tray of buns made from the flour. Danny Fisher took two and licked them both. Miss West said, "Not two Danny. Give one of those to Rosie."
I didn't want one.
I didn't want a bun that <u>he'd</u> licked.
        Love from Ginger.

Dear Aunty Mabel,
  The teachers made a rope swing across the stream today and everyone had a go, except Sarah. I tried and tried but couldn't get over. I kept landing in the water.
  Roland Roberts said, "Rule number one: don't get wet!"
  Everybody laughed, but I didn't think it was very funny.
  I think I've got a cold.

  Love R.

Dear Grandad,

It's stopped raining at last and we're going to sleep in the tents tonight. Yippee! Now Sarah says she doesn't want to because there may be creepy crawlies. Miss West told her that nothing could possibly harm her.

Danny Fisher said, "Only slugs and snails and spiders and snakes!"

Sarah started to cry and Danny had to see Mr Granville.

I hope there aren't any crawlies.

Love from Rosie.

Dear Mum,
  We've just been to a blacksmiths to watch him shoe a horse. When the shoe went on the horse's hoof it was still hot, but it didn't hurt him. You could smell the hoof burning. It was horrible.
  Mr Bennet said, "It smells like Mr Granville's socks."
  Guess what? When we got outside the sun was shining.
  I think we've got sausages for tea.

  Love from Rosie.

Dear Grandad,
    We woke up so early this morning. It was still dark. We lay in our beds talking until it got light and the birds started singing. Miss Jones said, "O.K. girls, who's going to help me make breakfast?"
We all yelled ME. We made eggy-bread. It's fab!
I'm getting used to camp now.
                    Love from Ginger Nut.

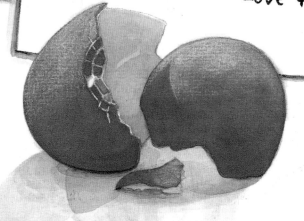

Dear Aunty Mabel,
  After tea today we built a big camp fire.
Mr Granville played his guitar and we all sat
round and sang songs. We stayed up really
late until all the wood had burned away.

Miss West said, "Come on sleepy-heads, off
to the land of nod."

She let us go to bed without a wash.

I really like this camp.

Love from R.

Dear Mum,
 I did it! I crossed the stream on the rope and Mr Granville gave me a star. After lunch we're going to make a raft from logs and tomorrow we're going to visit some caves. I can't wait. Danny Fisher said, "Come on, Tarzan. It's my turn next."
I'm having the best holiday ever. Wish you were here.
            Lots of love from
                   Rosie. X

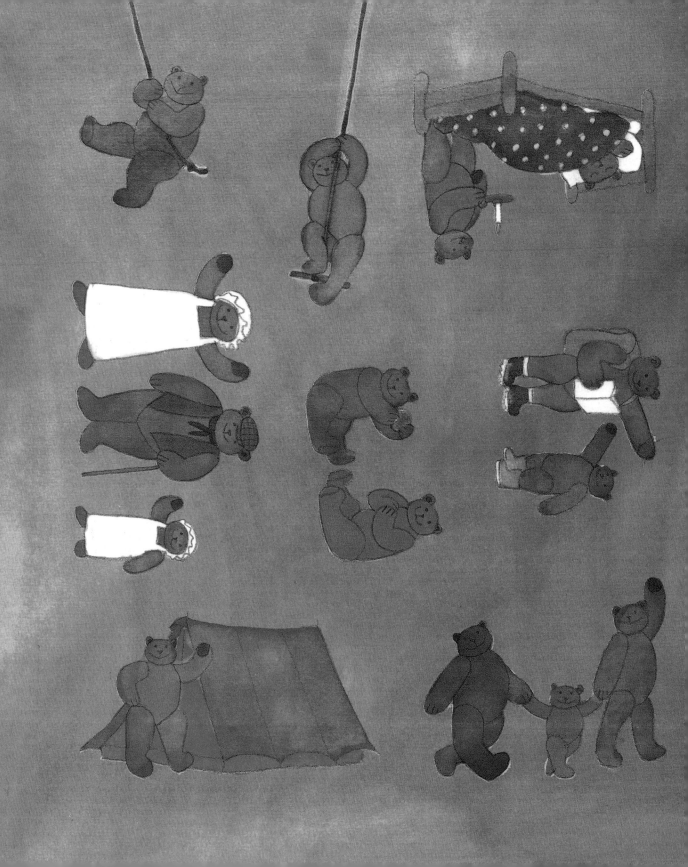

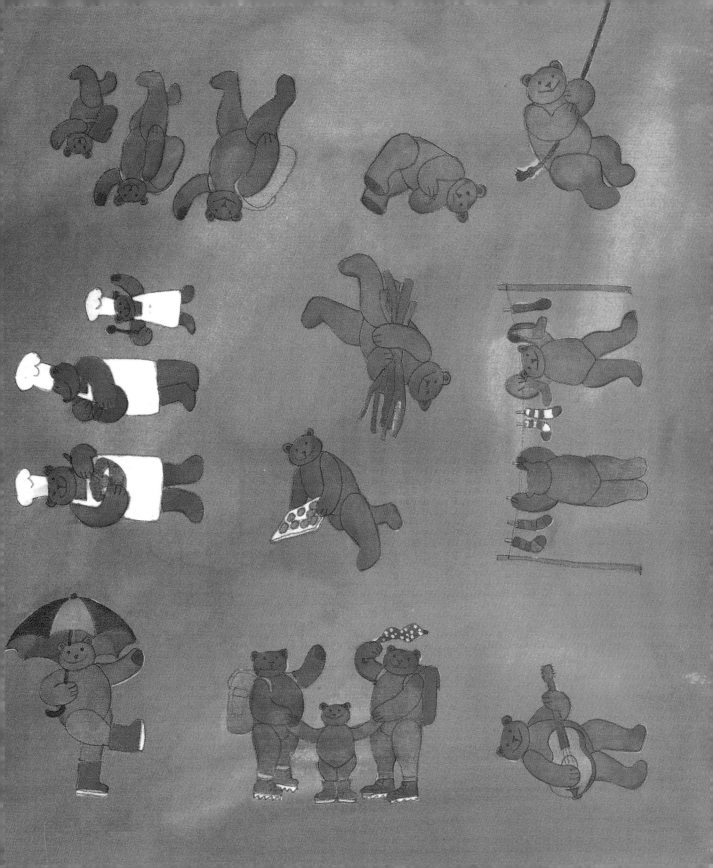

Some
bestselling Red Fox
picture books

THE BIG ALFIE AND ANNIE ROSE STORYBOOK
by Shirley Hughes
OLD BEAR
by Jane Hissey
OI! GET OFF OUR TRAIN
by John Burningham
DON'T DO THAT!
by Tony Ross
NOT NOW, BERNARD
by David McKee
ALL JOIN IN
by Quentin Blake
THE WHALES' SONG
by Gary Blythe and Dyan Sheldon
JESUS' CHRISTMAS PARTY
by Nicholas Allan
THE PATCHWORK CAT
by Nicola Bayley and William Mayne
WILLY AND HUGH
by Anthony Browne
THE WINTER HEDGEHOG
by Ann and Reg Cartwright
A DARK, DARK TALE
by Ruth Brown
HARRY, THE DIRTY DOG
by Gene Zion and Margaret Bloy Graham
DR XARGLE'S BOOK OF EARTHLETS
by Jeanne Willis and Tony Ross
WHERE'S THE BABY?
by Pat Hutchins